The Storm in the Barn

THE STORM IN THE BARN

MATT PHELAN

CANDLEWICK PRESS

Copyright © 2009 by Matt Phelan

First paperback edition 2011

Library of Congress Cataloging-in-Publication Data is available.

Library of Congress Catalog Card Number 2008938396

ISBN 978-0-7636-3618-0 (hardcover)
ISBN 978-0-7636-5290-6 (paperback)

11 12 13 14 15 16 SCP 10 9 8 7 6 5 4 3 2 1

Printed in Humen, Dongguan, China

This book was typeset in Agenda Light Italic.
The illustrations were done in pencil, ink, and watercolor.

Candlewick Press
99 Dover Street
Somerville, Massachusetts 02144

visit us at www.candlewick.com

For my dad,
who shared his love of stories

Every theory of the course of events in nature is necessarily based on some process of simplification of the phenomena and is to some extent therefore a fairy tale.

—Sir Napier Shaw, *Manual of Meteorology*

The dust can have it.

15

Jack, are you all right?

— What were you doing out there?

I was in town but . . . but . . .

Why didn't you take shelter at the general store?

Very interesting. You chose to run into the dust storm. That's not a rational decision —

I was running away from the dust, not into it.

Sometimes we think things — maybe even hear voices in our heads — that seem to make sense, seem to be the way things are. Isn't that right, Jack?

I . . . don't follow you, sir.

Your daughter's condition — which, by the by, our colleagues at the Red Cross headquarters in Wichita are now calling dust pneumonia — has . . . has not improved, Mrs. Clark. In fact —

Jack, see to your sisters. —

Did you really outrun the storm?
You must be the fastest boy in town.

No . . . I wouldn't say that.

I dunno.
You must be pretty fast.

I'm fast, too!

"At the time the wind began to blow, a ship was sailing far out upon the waters. When the waves began to tumble and toss and to grow bigger and bigger the ship rolled up and down, and tipped sidewise—first one way and then the other—and was jostled around so roughly that even the sailor-men had to hold fast to the ropes and railings to keep themselves from being swept away by the wind or pitched headlong into the sea."

"And the clouds were so thick in the sky that the sunlight couldn't get through them; so that the day grew dark as night, which added to the terrors of the storm."

We don't have a choice anymore. Do you think I want to leave our home? We just . . . we don't have a choice.

There's only so much I can do alone. Jack's no help.

The problem is this land. It's cursed.

I'll fix the car. Then we'll . . . go.

"I'm thinking of calling it dust dementia."

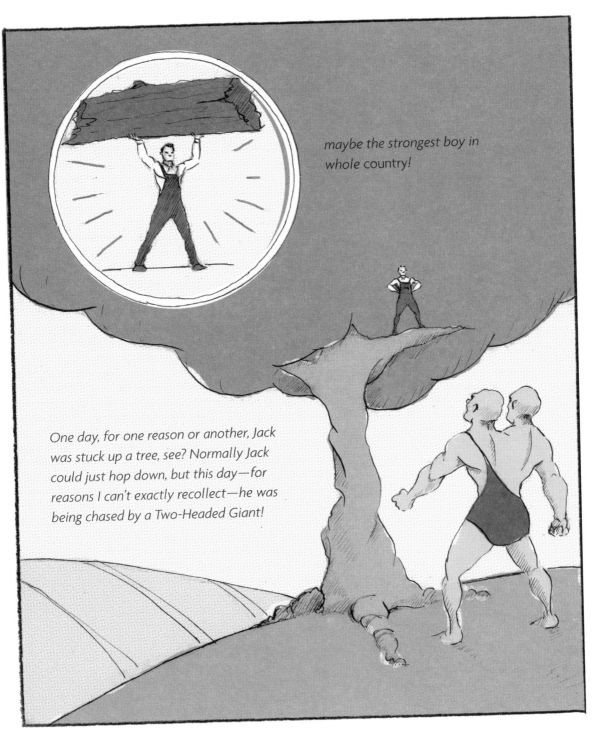

maybe the strongest boy in whole country!

One day, for one reason or another, Jack was stuck up a tree, see? Normally Jack could just hop down, but this day—for reasons I can't exactly recollect—he was being chased by a Two-Headed Giant!

Yep. Two-Headed Giant. —

So Jack cleverly outwitted the Giant by squeezing milk from an ordinary stone.

— Milk from a stone?

Yes, well, it was a trick of some sort.

Something about Jack having some milk — hidden in his jacket, then faking the whole thing with the rock.

Anyhoo! —

Eventually, Jack climbed down to face the Giant!

55

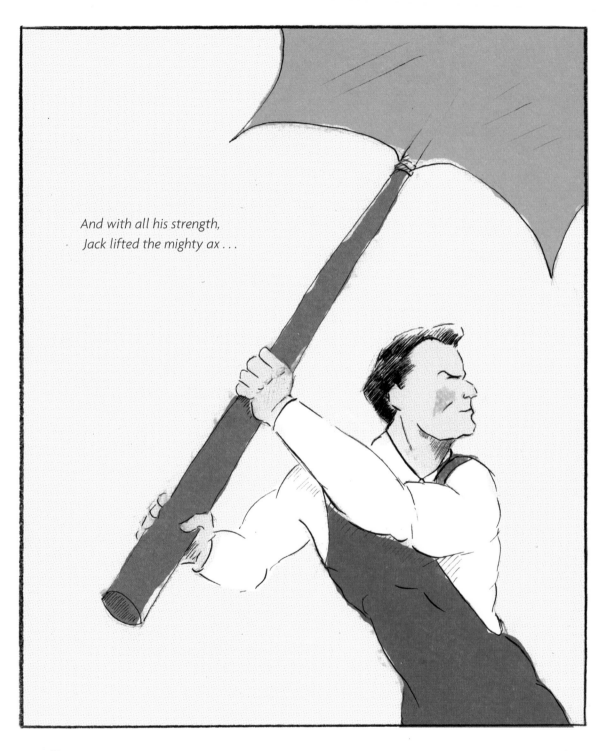

And with all his strength,
Jack lifted the mighty ax . . .

LATER

creeeak

splish

LATER

This is a good one. Dorothy is about to be set upon by Wheelers . . . men with four wheels instead of hands and feet.

Oh.

What did you do today, Jack? Any adventures? See any Wheelers?

No . . .
I suppose not.

I was in the Talbots' abandoned barn. I didn't break in or any-thing—it's just that the door was stuck and I . . . Anyways . . .

It smelled funny.

Barns generally do.

No. Not like that. Not like animals. It smelled like . . . I don't know . . . a funny smell.

COUGH!
COUGH!

So . . . what is Dorothy up to?

Well, Dorothy was going to visit her uncle, and her ship was caught in a storm. She fell overboard with this chicken, but they both washed up in Oz. She's in the Deadly Desert now.

Is that wizard in this one?

Nope.

I know that Dorothy was taken out of Kansas by a twister, but I never understood why the wizard was in Oz. Was he running away? Was he hiding out? Like a gangster? Like Al Capone?

The wizard's not like Al Capone.

I know, but was he hiding out in Oz?

No. I suppose that in Oz he was a big wizard, more than just a fella. He wanted to be special, to be powerful.

an ocean of grass.

The Indians had it first. Acres of pastureland.

Then the white folks moved them out and started ranching.

But it was good land. It promised crops. Folks came from all over to farm it.
My family came early.

We lived in a dugout at first.
Right in the ground. Dirt walls.
Lots of bugs.

—Bugs?

Big bugs. It wasn't perfect, but it gave us shelter.

My daddy and my brothers worked harder than anyone.

They planted wheat . . .

and the wheat came up.

the dust came.
And the rain vanished.

I remember rain.

You're too young.
You've never even seen rain.

You were no older than seven
when the last rain fell, Jack.
So I wouldn't be too hard
on Mabel.

Yes, ma'am.

I love the planting season, when the rain comes.

But my favorite thing about the rain . . .

is right before it comes.

There is a certain smell in the air.

What the hell are you doing out here in the middle of the night?

– Mabel.

SLAM!

You got older, but the farm didn't. The dust stopped everything—except you getting older. It's not your fault that there was nothing for you to do, nothing for you to show us how valuable you are to the farm.

Dorothy . . .

No, I've thought about this, Jack. Mabel was just a squirt—still is. But you . . . When the rain went away, it took away your chance to grow up.

cough!

c-cough!

127

133

~ This must end.

"Westward the fertile Land of Ev suddenly ended a little way from the palace, and the girl could see miles and miles of sandy desert that stretched further than her eyes could reach."

"It was this desert, she thought, with much interest . . ."

"that alone separated her from the wonderful Land of Oz . . ."

"and she remembered sorrowfully that she had been told no one had ever been able to cross this dangerous waste but herself."

"Once a cyclone had carried her across it, and a magical pair of silver shoes had carried her back again."

"But now she had neither a cyclone nor silver shoes to assist her . . ."

"and her condition was sad indeed."

150

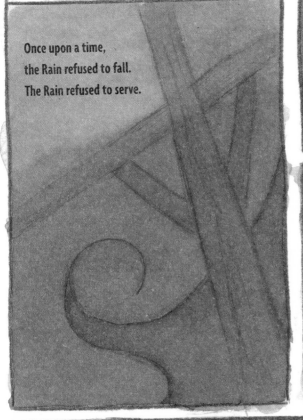

Once upon a time,
the Rain refused to fall.
The Rain refused to serve.

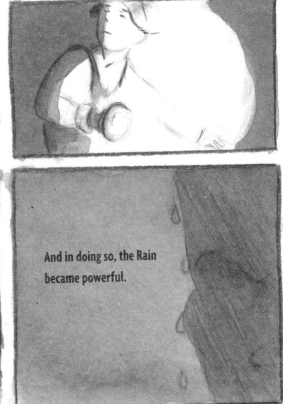

And in doing so, the Rain
became powerful.

Poor brave, *useless* boy.

WHAM!

Boy . . .

Where there is thunder . . .
the rain must surely follow.

181

We're staying here.
We're going to bring the crops back.
And Jack . . .

Jack, I could sure
use your help.

AUTHOR'S NOTE

FIFTEEN YEARS AGO, I was prowling through a used bookstore, not searching for anything in particular. The book that caught my eye was a slim paperback by Donald Worster called *Dust Bowl: The Southern Plains in the 1930s.* It was a full account of the Dust Bowl years—the various causes, the impact on the people, the implications for the future. The selling point for me, however, was the photography.

I had seen some of these photos before. As a kid, I poured over my dad's oversized hardback volumes of Works Progress Administration (WPA) photography. The stark black-and-white images captured by Dorothea Lange, Arthur Rothstein, Walker Evans, and others grabbed my attention. It was the faces. Against a backdrop of a vanishing farmland, these faces stared at the camera with haunting directness. They were beaten down, but somehow they weren't yet beaten.

Ten years ago, I watched an *American Experience* documentary called "Surviving the Dust Bowl." It included actual film footage—not just still photos—of massive dust clouds covering whole towns, people scrambling for cover, and even a brutal jackrabbit drive. This last event still haunted survivors of the time who, now in their old age, were interviewed for the documentary. This was what struck me most. I began to imagine what the experience of living in the Dust Bowl must have been like through the eyes of a kid. Without the complicated expla-nation of the history of over-planting, soil erosion, and other factors, a young boy or girl would only know a world that could suddenly vanish in a moving mountain of dark dust. The rain had gone away. But where?

Five years ago, for reasons I can't explain, I sketched a tall, dark, sinister figure with a face like a thunderstorm.

I knew I wanted this book to be a story set in the Dust Bowl but not a story directly about the Dust Bowl. I wanted to bring in elements of American folklore, like the Jack tales that were still being told and the Oz books that had been enthralling kids for thirty-odd years at that point. In the next two years, *The Wizard of Oz* would become a movie and Superman would leap from the pages of comic books, but in 1937 there were mostly just stories — stories a boy in Kansas would think about as he looked at a land apparently as cursed as any in the fairy tales.

Many years have passed since I first discovered those iconic photographs. They still have the power to stop me cold when-ever I see them. I went back to those photos many times during the making of this book. Each time, I tried to absorb some small feeling for that strange era, so that I could tell this Dust Bowl story with pictures of my own.

Three Stories of
One Extraordinary Journey

Around the World

written and illustrated by
Matt Phelan

═══════════════════════

At the end of the nineteenth century, The Challenge
beckons. Fraught with peril, a new adventure at every
turn, and the chance at celebrity, three real-life figures
set out to circumnavigate the globe. 1884: Thomas
Stevens declares he will accomplish the journey . . .
on a bicycle. 1890: Intrepid journalist Nellie Bly sets
out to break Jules Verne's fictional record and return
home within eighty days. 1895: Joshua Slocum sets
out on a 35-foot sloop to become the first person to
sail around the world alone. Three tales unfold in this
graphic novel about the greatest journey on Earth.

═══════════════════════

www.candlewick.com